AF761311

आँchal

RUBAL CHOUDHARY

(Compiler)

Book*Squirrel* Publication

Regd. Under MSME Act.

“***अाँchal***”

By: Rubal Choudhary

Cover design by – Mr.Ash

ISBN: 978-93-89106-77-0

Poems and Open Letteers

1st Edition

Price:

Disclamer

This Anthology is a fiction. The compiler has tried best to edit and curate the content of the co-authors and is made plagiarism free.

All the Write ups in this book are unique.

In case of any plagiarism detected, neither the compiler, nor the publishers are responsible. Co - authors will be solely responsible for their own content.

Acknowledgement

The making of this Anthology would not have been possible without the co-authors. A gratitude towards all who have worked hard and have made effort for this book to be a success.

I am thankful to BookSquirrel Publications without whom this project would not be possible.

Above all, the hearthy thanks to our parents, family and friends for supporting us throughout this project. Lastly, we thank the almighty for giving us this opportunity and strength to complete it successfully.

Compiler

Rubal Choudhary

This is Rubal Choudhary from Gurgaon, Haryana. She is 19-year-old and currently pursuing English Hons. from Delhi University. She aspires to become an IAS officer. She is a content writer and a co- author in many

Anthologies.
She recently compiled an anthology named- "Medley of Words" and "Miracles from Heaven".

Earlier,

writing was not a cup of tea for her but later she realised that she can write too. She loves to research and write articles of different Genres. She is good in making sketches and paintings and reads novels.

She believes write until it suits as natural as to respire.

To my loving mother,

First of all, Thank you for being my mother. I know, I have never thanked you for anything. Words can never express your love and care towards me. I could never thank you for showing me what eternal love is. Whenever you are around, each and everything feels calm and smooth.

You have always been a constant support and a backbone to me. I could not thank you for anything, be it teaching me lessons when needed, lifting me when I was low and many more. Thank you for staying with me and I know you will never leave me. You deserve every single happiness in this world. You are the most important person in my life.

Thank you for always becoming my friend and please remain the same throughout the life.

What all your haven't done for me- you have cried, you have fought, you have loved and most importantly you have smiled. I would like to tell you, you are the strongest woman I have ever met. God has given me everything, but this blessing, I would not be able to forget. You have sacrificed your life to me, be it when I have cried you have cried, when I have laughed you have laughed, when I have enjoyed you have enjoyed. You owned it without showing and realizing anything.

Thank you for listening to me always!

Lastly, Thank you for being the best mother.

Your loving daughter

Rubal

I am so blessed to have you.

You not only love me, you keep me safe everytime

I really think life comes with a mother not with a destiny planned.

I always want to dedicate this song to you-

"तू कितनी अच्ची है,

तू कितनी भोली है,

प्यारी प्यारी है,

ओ माँ, ओ माँ, ओ माँ, ओ माँ ।"

"Motherhood"= not only a 9 letter word i.e. short right!

but it's worth having experience.

Being a mother is not easy, it is about learning those strengths which you didn't know.

What all I am today, is just because you.

Thank you so much mummy!

ANAMIKA SHUKLA

Anamika Shukla from Uttar Pradesh but presently in Bhubaneswar . Writing is her passion and a means to express her emotions.She is a hardworking, emerging and a confident girl .Her works are based on reality having a positive aspect.She is an optimistic and a responsible person completion all her works with patience and dedication.

मेरी दुनिया– माँ

मेरी दुनियाँ है तुझसे और तू ही मेरा जहाँन है माँ

तेरे जैसा कोई और कहाँ है माँ|

खुदा से पहले तेरे ही सजदे में सर झुकता है माँ

मेरा जहाँ मुकम्मल हो जाये जो इक बार तू हँस दे माँ|

जिन्दगी में संघर्ष बहोत हैं और कड़े इसके

इम्तहान हैं माँ

पर बहोत राहत महसूस होता है तेरे आँचल के

छाँव में माँ|

इस जहां में ऐश-ओ-आराम के बहोत बंदोबस्त हैं माँ

पर मुझे सुकून बस तेरी गोद ही देती है माँ

भले ही सब मुझसे रुठ जायें चाहे सारे बंधन टूट जायें माँ

इक तेरा दामन ना छुटे बस इतनी सी इल्तज़ा है माँ।

तुम सब जानती हो माँ

कभी जो रुठ जाऊँ तुमसे

बच्चा समझ कर मना लेती हो माँ|

तुमसे कुछ ना भी कहूँ मैं

तो भी सबकुछ जान लेती हो माँ|

अपना दर्द भले ही तुमसे मैं छुपाऊँ

पर आँखों से तुम सबकुछ पढ़ लेती हो माँ|

ऐसा हुनर कहाँ से है तुम में

जो मन की बातें भी जान लेती हो माँ|

तेरे हाँथ के खाने में जो स्वाद है

उसके आगे सब निस्वाद है माँ

किस्मत बुलंद है मेरी तू जो मेरे पास है माँ

ईश्वर हर जगह नहीं आ सकता इसलिए

मुझे माँ से नवाजा है माँ।

ANJALEE GARG

This is anjalee from Delhi. She is persuing B.A. English honours from Amity University Noida. Writing is her passion since middle school. For her it's a way to pour out ones emotions. Writing is the thing by which she is able to connect to numerous people and to reach more and more hearts.

मा, जानते हो मतलब इस शब्द का?
कहना आसान है कि वो उसकी मा है!
दर्द जानते हो कितना सहा उसने,
सिर्फ सुनने के लिए शब्द "मा"!
रातों को तपते बुखार में इसने मुझे संभाला है,
सुबह को उठकर प्यार से मेरा वो माथा उसने सहलाया है!
शायद भूल है में,
शायद भूल जाऊ में कि तू मेरा परमात्मा है!
लेकिन मा तो वो है जिसका हाथ बेशक से बिना हिज़क तुम जिटक दो,
लेकिन वो तो दुआओं में यही मांगती है कि आखिरी सासों में भी मेरी औलाद का हाथ मेरे हाथ में हो!
ऐसे ही उसको मा नहीं बोलता में,
उसने भी बड़े नाज़ों से पाला है मुझे!
बचपन की तरह आज भी उसने है तो मेरे आसुओं को पोछा है!
दर्द हुआ था तुम्हारे सीने में?
नहीं ना?
वो रोई मुझे रोता देख, शायद इसलिए सिर्फ में उसको ही बोलता हूं "मा"!
नाकामयाब हूं मेशायाद तुझे अभी खुश रखने में,
लेकिन ये दिल भी रोता है देख तुझे इस दुख में!
दुआ है आज कि ए खुदा कर दे इतना काबिल मुझे की दुनिया कि सबसे खूबसूरत चीज का ऐतबार भी रोके ना "मेरी मा की मुस्कुराहट!"
मेरा साथ नहीं पर,
मेरे हर जज़्बात में तो तू है मा!

आँchal

तू थी तो ज़िन्दगी आसान थी,

ज़्यादा कुछ ना कर पाई, तब भी तो तू साथ निभाती थी मा!

लेकिन मैं आज कामयाब भी तो तेरी वजह से हूं,

तेरा वो साथ ही तो कुछ कर गुजरने का हौसला देता था मा!

बात नहीं होती तुमसे अब,

लेकिन ज़िन्दगी के मायने भी तो तुझसे ही सीखा हूं में मा!

दूर रह कर भी तुझसे प्यार कम नहीं होता,

तू साथ नहीं पर एहसास तो है मा!

लफ़्ज़ों में बयान करना तेरा मेरा! रिश्ता नामुमकिन सा है,

बस इतना समझ ले तू है तो खुशियां हैं मा!

याद बहुत आती है तेरी,

रात आसुओं में निकल जाती है मा!

तेरे आँचल में लिपट कर सोना,

वो सुकून कि नींद अब नहीं आती मा!

तेरी हाथों से पेट भर रोटीयां खाना,

वेसी भूक अब नहीं लगती मा!

तेरी कमी तो मुझे हर पल सताती है,

एक तू ही तो थी जो मेरा हर पल साथ निभाती है!

ANJANA AGARWAL

This is Anjana Agarwal. Writing has been her way of expression since she was small. Its bcz writing gives her happiness. Born and brought up in Shillong, married in Kolkata, its through words that she portray emotions best. Insta handle: anjana54

Hey Maa.....

It's been so many years but I never thanked or talked about you.

Maa is that word which I think no one can describe in words.. as a mom myself, i will say i know what is maa. what is her value in life. I remember when i was small, mom use to take care of me. Always used to give me good clothes. I was her pari. She used to only scold me for my studies. But i can say, till my mom taught me, I scored highest in class and everyone use to praise me. I felt so proud but never understood it was for my mom I am getting these praises. As i grew up, my mom told me: now as you have grown up, do your own studies. I will not always be there for you. do by yourself. I thought wow! I am free.. I will study by myself. No one will say me anything or scold me.But, as I saw I was degrading in my class and teachers also started ignoring me, and I became a low student. Then, I realized that when mom use to teach me, I was the best student in school. I started regretting why mom left to teach me.

But mom wanted me to stand me own my feet. This how I completed my studies.After that I got engaged. I was so nervous, I was like I have to leave my mom and go. I was terrified.. without mom? nooo, Oh god please.. I can't live without her. But she taught me she was also girl and left her mom and dad and got married, and has to adjust to everything. She told me girls have to adjust. I thought, before engagement, my mom never told me that a girl has to adjust. She use to give me what i wanted, and fulfilled all my wishes, even more then my brothers.

They used to get jealous of me but my mom used to say I will fulfill all my daughters wishes. It was like I am on top of the world, but suddenly as i got engaged she started talking about adjusting. I was again surprised! Why ma is saying this? But this i realized when i got married. I had to face many problems and it was my mom who supported me in every path of my life. And said whatever the situation, you have to adjust and make your family happy. She never taught me anything wrong. That is why i am happy in my family and adjusted well with all ups and downs.

My mom is mom whom i can never repay.As my mom, i got a good mother in law too. In the beginning, I was afarid of her, as she was strick and used to stay less at home. But she was very sweet also. Never binded me with any rituals, that you have to do. So, I never had to do many things that many people has to in there in-laws place. She even made me strong. she told me you have to be strong and take care of your family.Either be it mother by blood, or mother by mere relation, mothers are the best.

I love you maa.

Your Mili

ANKUMONI DAS

She is Ankumoni Das from Goalpara Assam. Current She stays in Guwahati. She is currently pursuing degree in Microbiology.

MAA , How are you ?

You always say , "you are fine" . But don't seem like that . You always remain gloomy and fragile these days . You always stay lost and silent . You don't even talk to me or dad . "Why is it so ?" . I miss you , "MAA" . I miss "the strict you" . I miss the "angry bird" in you . I miss the jolly you . You were the most "enthusiastic" person in our family but now everything changed .

There were days when you used to be with me like "the shadow" . And now its like in a week we used to talk twice or thrice . You were the strongest pillar of the family . But now as you are sick everything seems falling apart . Its very difficult for me to see you like this .

MAA , I love you so much , but I am very bad at expressing. I used to get angry with you very soon , scold you too for not taking your medicines or taking all those unhealthy things . And my harsh talks makes you more sad . I am sorry for all that . MAA I never want to hurt you . Memories with you are irreplaceable . I still remember the HS days . You were woke till 2 to 3 am with me . Again in the morning you woke up early , finish your household works quickly and make me revise everything . From making notes to draw diagrams for practicals you did everything you could . The most sweetest memory was you didn't have any idea about mathematics than also you used to sit beside me and match the answers from the tuition copy.And the most exciting were you used to surprise me with new clothes every month . I still remember you gifted me my first green eyepencil and now you don't even ask from where do I buy my stuffs.You were not only my mother , you were my friend , my protector , my teacher in short everything .

When I got bored during study hours , you used to take me out for walks and we used to talk about everything . You used to take me to dance classes and scold me as I used to gossip a lot instead of practising.Your disease took away the cheerful nature of yours which I do miss a lot . But I am happy that you are recovering and I hope to see you as you were 15 years ago. You too are not good in expressing your love but I know on those stormy nights you put the blanket on me and give me always the huge part of the evening snacks. The best part of my life is that I am your daughter. It is said that God can't be with everyone at all times so God has blessed us with our parents .

But for me , God is 24*7 with me , in the form of my parents .One whose love and affection can't be compared with anything of the world not even with the pleasure of heaven.

Dad being the pillar of my life and Mom being the concrete of that pillar !!

Yours Anku

ANTHONY COLACO

Anthony colaco is 24, hailing from the beautiful dream destination along the West coast 'Goa'. He is Marketing sales Executive by Profession.He is keen of Music. It was unexpected that he started writing & made it his passion now cause he says" Playing with words and nourishing to this beautiful universe can change the world in an unique way."

You can connect with him on Instagram:@acolaco_writes

The Extraordinary Universal Star - MOM

That day,when everything seems lost she fought like a true warrior for you to bring the everlasting dreamlight.

A star whose love is unimaginable and never ending like a dazzling sunlight.

That day, when life seems completely disgraceful she made sure you see today an infinite grace.

A star god shooted down to the earth who always guides you in your life's destructive race. That day,When unknowingly everything seems degraded in no time she showed a pathway you always destined.

A star that will be the greatest universal champion that creator ever created.

" MOM- the Real Gem in everyone's life & favourite Soul who always deserve a millions time applause. "

ASHUTOSH DAS

Ashutosh Das, born on 10th Oct '98 in Bihar and brought up in M.P and currently settled in Indore. He is pursuing a Degree in B. Visual Arts. For him, writing is eternal love. A writer, Author, Compiler, Storyteller, Poet, and a performer. He is just walking and trying to make roads for coming writers easy!

A word which makes the love seems Unnatural,

A word which carries whole world in itself,

A word that defines the Life!

Yes

The word *Maa*

Which make the Scarifies seems so easy,

The one who can make the whole world shake

Just for the sake of her child!

There have been lot of moments where

I have been asked Why haven't you wrote on Maa

Even my own Mom said

"You Writings are always of & for ofDad, am nothing to you !'

To which I want to write

That Maa

There is lot to write on you , for you,

But when ever I write

My pen never supports saying

"the one who made the words to her I can't make words for!'

Well, It is right also,

How in the world any one can make word

When that one above all sitting up in sky,

Even he can't say a word in front MAA.

Just want to say

You are reason for us be to alive

You are the reason to make me a Man

You are the one who gave love a true meaning

And Everyday I want just to see a smile on you....

क्योंकि मैंने मां को मेरे लिए पापा की जगह लेते देखा है

हां मैंने भी कुछ रिश्तो को बड़े करीब से देखा है!!

AVANI SINGHAL

She is Avani Singhal. She is a Art and a food lover .An introvert who loves to write.

"माँ "

तेरा ही तो अंश हूँ मैं।

तेरी ही तो जान हूँ तूने ही सिखाया दुनिया में जीना

सयानी बनाके ज़माने में चलना|

जब लड़खड़ाई तूने ही संभाला प्यार से हमेशा तूने ही तो पुकारा। तूने ही बिगाड़ा मुझे तूने ही संवारा है|

तू ही तो एक मेरा सहारा है। तू ही तो हिफाजत मेरी।

तू ही इबादत तूने ही तो हमेशा प्यार की बाहों में पाला है|

दुःख में तुझे देख कर मैं चेन से कैसे बैठूंगी|

तेरा हर आंसू देखकर मैं अंदर ही अंदर तड़पुँगी।

तू कहती नहीं कभी तो क्या तेरे हर जज्बात से वाक़िफ़ हूँ।

जताया नहीं कभी मैंने पर मैं तुझसे इस दुनिया में सबसे ज्यादा प्यार करती हूँ।

तुझे ही अपना पूरा संसार समझती हूँ ।

AYUSHI JAWANPURIA

Ayushi Jawanpuria a freelance poet born in the season of summer in the month of April . She is attracted towards the contents related to love , life and family . Her poems portray her experiences and feelings towards her love and heartbreak. She has penned her feelings and her happiness beautifully in this anthology. Her view towards life is beautifully expressed with other passionate writers.

<u>मां</u>

जन्म से पहले हमसे जो प्यार करे,वह होती है मां।

भूख लगे तो जो अपने हाथों से खाना खिलाए,वह होती है मां।

हमारे आंखो के आंसू अपने आंखो में जो ले ले,वह होती है मां।

जो बीमार होने पर भी अपने बच्चों का खयाल रखे,वह होती है मां।

अपने सपने मार कर, जो दूसरो के सपनों को पूरा करे,वह होती है मां।

खुद भुखे रह कर जो अपने परिवार का पेट भरे,वह होती है मां।

अपना दर्द तो सब बयान कर लेते हैं, पर जो अपना दर्द कभी न बयान करे,वह होती है मां।

पिता के डांट फटकार से जो बचाएं,वह होती है मां।

हर दर्द को जो खुशी खुशी बरदाश करे,वह होती है मां।

पापा कि परी से दादा दादी की लाडली, भाई की अभिमान
से एक पत्नी का सफर तय करती है,और फिर बनती है
वह मां।

हम सब गुस्से में न जाने क्या कुछ नहीं बोल देते,

पर हमें डांट कर, समझा कर जो प्यार करती है,

वह होती है मां।

मां! मैं जानती हूं मैं वैसी नहीं जैसा तुम मुझे बनाना
चाहती थी,

पर मैं आपसे बहुत प्यार करती हूं मां।

भगवान से बस एक ही दुआ है,

तू हमेशा खुश रहे, सलामत रहे।

Hello mumma,

How are you? I'm fine here , hope you are fine there. I'm writing this letter to tell you that how much I miss you. I miss our old golden days mum when we used to play together, dance together, laugh together, cry together. I miss everything mum. Now when I'm out of town for my studies, far away from you, I miss the taste of yummy dishes made by you. I miss our fights when I used to come late from my tution and you used to scold me. And I used to fight that why are you scolding, and fight with you. Remember after that you used to feed me.. I miss those things mumma. You know you are not only my mum, but a friend, a mentor, a doctor, a teacher, everything for me. You are the bestest mother in this whole universe. No one can become like you. I seriously adore you a lot and I really don't know what I have done without you. Truly blessed to be your daughter. And when I'll become a mum one day, I want to be like you, I want to share our stories with my children, our memories of laugh, cry, everything. Your teaching and values are the only asset which I have with me for the lifetime and will always with me whatever the situation is. You said it very true that I'm gonna miss my home and food badly ones I'm far away from home for my studies or job and I used to laugh at it. But at the end you proved to be correct. And your decisions, whether I like it or not, it always proved to be correct. And that chocolate cake, made by you...ohh my god...I miss that very badly. No one can make that chocolate cake like you make. I'm falling short of words and I really don't know how to express my feelings because you know I'm very bad at these things. I just want to say I love you and I miss you.

By your crazy daughter,

Vashu

BINDIYA AMETHIYA

This is Bindiya Amethiya. She is 35 yrs. She has done her studies in B.pharma, MBA and is a Housewife. She has recently encountered passion for words and can give voice to any subject.

MOTHER

A person

from unconditional flowing

love,can rely on..

forever

fulfilling thirst

nurturer,transformer seeds

to a blooming enormous

tree!

witnesses to

cherishes to each

seasons each chapter of

life

passing by

stands by our

side in Any storms,

tragedy

life throws

to us. feelings

emotions living within us

from

the first

breathe To our

divine ultimate journey called

DEATH

-wings

DHIVYA AYNAN

She is Dhivya,a South Indian,who loves art and literature to the core. She thinks "If I could express everything, I wouldn't have started writing!"

Dearest mom.,

I'm the most luckiest girl existing in this world.Do you know why? A mom can never be so friendly to her child that she feels courageous enough to share all the stuffs.At times,you might have felt that you've failed to be a responsible mother.On the contrary,you've been the best mom and you'll always be.When I stumbled,you gave me all the courage to face the world.No matter what I do,you'll always accept me for who I'm and you would never judge me. How could your love be so unconditional that I always feel blessed? How could you be so unselfish that you've never thought about yourself ? I've never seen god but I've felt how a god's love would be.I feel blessed.I really have no words to thank you.You know what? You are somewhat different from other Indian mothers.You gave all the freedom that a girl needs and you knew that I would never misuse the freedom that you've given to me.You are the reason for my boldness,you are the reason for my happiness,you are my everything! You always wanted to raise me up as a revolutionary women and I'm just being the way that you wished. Dearest 'Gundachi';I love you.There might be trillions of obstacles in front of me,just remember that I'm not afraid of facing those hitches. As a mother.,you've given your best.I'm your daughter,right? I'll really bring about a change in this society and I'll always be the revolutionary women as you wished. I'll bring laurels to you.I love you and only you,no one else!

--Your little fairy

HARSH BHADORIYA

He is Harsh Bhadoriya from Ahmedabad. He started writing from last one year and today he is a part and co-author of many anthology. Writing wasn't his passion but today people call him by a tag "WRITER" For reading his write-ups do follow his Instagram: @bharsh06

माँ

माँ कहूं उसे या मम्मी कहूं।

पैर चुमू उसके या उसकी रोज पूजा करू।

वो तो शरदी के मौसम में जैसे खिली धूप है।

माँ तो एक देवता का रूप है।।

अमीर हो या गरीब।

माँ तो मा होती है।

देख के अपने बच्चो को तकलीफ में।

परेशान तो हर माँ होती है।।

बच्चो के लिए वो शेफ बन जाती है।

उनकी छोटी-छोटी खुशियों के लिए हर मुश्किल पार कर जाती है।

बच्चे जब भी डर जाए, गोद में अपने वो सुलाती है।

अपने हिस्से का खाना भी वो बच्चो को खिलाती है।।

माँ के सामने रोने से बड़ा डर लगता है।

क्यूंकि जितना हम रोते है उससे ज्यादा उसका दिल रोता है।

वो हमे तों चुप करके सुला देती है।

फिर रात को वो छिप छिप के रोती है।

माँ-माँ कह कर पुरा घर सर पे उठा लेते है।

जब भी घर में आए "माँ कहाँ है" यही हम पूछते है।

बहुत अकेला लगता हे जब माँ का चेहरा नहीं दिखता।

चाहे कहीं भी घूम लो माँ के हाथ का खाना कही नहीं मिलता।।

माँ के प्यार को समझना तों नामुमकिन है।

हमारे जीवन में वो हमारा जिन है।

क्या लिखूं उसके लिए सब उसके लिए कम है।

कोई बयान ना कर सके माँ में इतने गुन है।।

अपनी रातो की नींद उड़ाके उसने हमे सुलाया है।

हमारी पढ़ाई के लिए खुद जाग कर हमे पढ़ाया है।

माँ तुम्हारा शुक्रिया कैसे अदा करू।

तुने तों हमे ज़िंदगी जीना सिखाया है।।

माँ.. तु हमारे लिए एक वरदान है।

माँ.. तु महान है।।

ISHANI AGARWAL

Born and brought up in Kolkata, she has done her schooling and collegefrom here itself. She is doing post graduation currently.

Ishani loves talking to people around, and is excited for this new beginning. Contact her on Insta- @ishani_agarwal_quotes

Dear Maa,

Taking this occasion, i would like to tell you so much. But talking about you, words are always less.So let me tell you how i feel, stuffs that come out of my heart...

There are times, when i am low, so low, that i want to give up on doing something. It is at that moment, that somehow mom always understands what i want, and is always ready with a solution.Be it something work related that i am stuck with, or be it an emotional breakdown, mom is always there.

Breakup tears are always shed in front of mom, and relationship joy is always celebrated with mom too.My constant in the whole world, who has stood by me despite me being at fault, though later made it a point to make me understand my mistake, has always been my mother.For me, she is the one reason why i am ready to take up any kind of challenge in life.

She is the strength behind my victories, and the weakness behind my fright.My reason to go on for so long, has been my mother, and she will always be the reason.

And i believe, somewhere or the other, this is applicable not only to me, but every child will be able to connect to this. Some point in their life, it is always mom, who is there to support you.

She is the only person who will never judge you no matter what you do. She will stand by you, holding you and supporting you.

Even if she lets you go at a time, it is only for you to stand at your own feet. So that someday if she is not there, you can do your things on your own.

When you get married off, or when even the talk of marriage comes up, she is the first to shed tears, coz for her, imagining a life without her daughter is difficult.Even if the whole world is against you, you will still find your mother beside you.

Maa,I may not say this that often,But you are my pillar of strength at all times..

Loves you to the moon and back..It is with you that I fight the most, but it is also you that I love the most.

ISHIKA AGARWAL

She is Ishika Agarwal . Being a class 10 student, her imagination

ran wild.She tried penning down her imaginations. She loves writing. It is nothing else but a passion.She is From Kolkata.

Insta handle: ishika_agarwal13

Mother's love

Mother's love is a totally different kind of love. I have a very sweet yet tangy kind of relationship with my mother . Whenever she gets angry, I too become very angry and irritated . But when she starts talking ill or gets upset , I am always there and cannot bear a single drop of tear in her eyes. Whenever I am ill she is always there to take care of me even when she is upset ,busy ,or herself not well. She is a person who even after taking care of me the whole day she can still wake up at night if needed . She never gets tired in the matter of family. She can be busy with work the whole day but when I need her, she is always there. Whenever I want to talk , she is always there. Even in the darkest times , she can joke just for our sake .she never tell us the problems that is going onn in her life . She gives us everything we want ,never have to say it twice . I don't know how but she always have the solution to every problem .

JASS

Jass, from New Delhi. He is an educated and self employed person. Firstly, he was a silent writer but his friends encouraged him to explore his skills. He started writting after he faced a dark phase in his life. Now, he has been published as a co-author in more than 3 anthologies

यह बेवफ़ाई लिखने वाली कलम,

न जाने माँ पर क्या लिखेगी ।।

जिस लहज़े में लिखती है यह

क्या उसमे मेरी माँ की सच्चाई दिखेगी ||

बदनाम तो करती है यह सबको बहुत, क्या मेरी माँ के नाम कुछ कर पायेगी।।

किया तो बहुत उसने मेरा,क्या यह मेरी कलम उसका कर्ज़ा चूका पायेगी ।।

चलो जो भी हो, मै आज माँ पर ही लिखूंगा,

कितनी लायक है मेरी कलम मेरी माँ के, आज बस यही देखूंगा ।।

न जाने इस जस्स को लिखना आता है या नहीं,

आज यह फ़ैसला हो जायेगा ।।

फिर उसी तरह मेरी शायरी का एक हिस्सा,

मेरी माँ का भी हो जायेगा ।।

समझाती है वो मुझे अक्सर, की तू अभी बच्चा है ।।

बहुत तेज़ हो गई है यह दुनियाँ, बाहर निकलने को तू अभी कच्चा है ।।

मगर क्या करूँ ना समझ हूँ, उसपे भड़क जाता हूँ ।।

करवाने को अपनी बात पूरी, उस से झगड़ जाता हूँ ।।

न जाने क्यों उसे बाहर जा कर भी, मुझे कुछ होता नहीं।।

शायद उसकी दुआ का ही असर है,

जो उसका नालायक उस से जुदा होता नहीं ।।

तुझे कभी बोल तो नहीं पाया, मगर कलम अपनी से हूँ वाकिफ बहुत,

आज कुछ न कुछ तो तेरे भी नाम करूंगा ।।

सर उठा कर चलेगी घमंड से तू, जस्स का वादा है तुझसे,

ऐसा कोई काम करूंगा||

KOHINUR ALI KHAN

Thia is Ramjan Ali Khan, He is a student of Banarhat Hindi govt. College. Indeed,most of the people known to him by "Kohinur" He mostly writes poems, stories, shayari His favourite hobby is cricket but when he started to hold pen in his hand, writing became his favourite hobby .

माँ की ममता

माँ ओ माँ मुझे प्यार से खिलाना बहुत दिन हो गया,
जी हाँ जब में रोता था छोटी -सी-छोटी बातो मैं,
हाँ माँ हाँ तेरा मनाना भी आज बहुत दिन हो गया
हाँ जब मैं सोता था चैन की नींद बेफिकर और
बेताहासा ,
अभी तलक याद है प्यारी-प्यारी लोरी मुझे सुनाया
करती थी,
हाँ माँ हाँ तेरे आँचल से छिपाना बहुत दिन हो गया|
वक्त पर मेरे साथ जबरजस्ती करना प्यार करना
ओर मुझसे रूठना, मेरे कपरे गोले हो जाए तो बदल
देना नाराजगी जाहिर करना,
हाँ माँ हाँ तेरे हाथ से खिलाना बहुत दिन हो गया|
मेरे ख्वाबो को हकीकत मैं बदलना चाहतो को
मुकम्मल बनाना, मेरे हर ज़िद पर प्यार और नरमी
से पेश आना हाँ माँ हाँ तेरे गोद पर सुलाना बहुत
दिन हो गया|

KSHITIJ GOUR

Kshitij Gour, born on 26th Dec '98 in Ujjain, M.P and currently settled in Indore. He is pursuing

a Degree in B.Sc Agriculture. He's is a writer and a poet. For him writing is an expression of love.

जो शब्दों में बांध ना सकूं, लाख कोशिशों के बाद भी जा ना सकूं|

कितना प्यार है तुमसे मा, ये जानते हुए भी बता ना सकूं|

तुम्हारे आंचल के कारण ही,आज अपने पैरों पर खड़ा हूं|

मैं आज भी वही बच्चा हूं,बस अब दिखने में थोड़ा बड़ा हूं|

चंदा मामा की लोरी हो या;हो रहा जी का घोड़ा

मेरी छोटी सी मुस्कान के लिए,तुमने कोई तरीका ना छोड़ा|

बिना मेरे बोले ही मेरी बातों को समझ जाती हो

कोई हो या ना हो, तुम हमेशा साथ हो मेरे इस बात का एहसास दिलाती हो...

सबकी चिंता तुम्हें खुद से ज़्यादा ही रहती है, मा ईश्वर का रूप है, ये सारी दुनिया तभी कहती है|

जिससे इस जीवन की शुरुआत हुई थी, उसी के साथ अंत चाहता हूं|

खुदा से एक ही दुआ है, अगले जन्म में तेरी ही कोक का आसरा चाहता हूं...

LAXMI MAURYA

Laxmi Maurya , studying in 12th standard in Canossa convent girls inter college faizabad , Uttarpradesh (India) . She loves writing poem and designing .

Mom

She cries when I cry

She laugh when I smile, She can walk 100 miles

For me in the sunlight, She remains hungry but feed me

I don't know how she reads me,

She sell her wishes for buying me gift, and buried her dreams for mine,

She can be in dark for lightning my life

She has wings but make me fly and hide her pain for my smile,

She has a life but never lived ,she can enjoy but she suffer,

She leaves her path and walk with me

She is not a teacher but teaches me all and stand with me in rise and fall,

Whose pleasure is my success and comfort is my happiness,

Whose love is only mine

And none can be as she

And she is my "MOM".

MOTE SHRAVANI

She is Mote Shravani.

She loves to write and mainly on peace.

Guiding Mom

Mom, From The Time I Was Really Young

I Realised I Had Someone....You, Who Always Cared,

Who Always Protected Me,

Who Was Always There For Me,

No Matter What. You Taught Me Every Right And

Wrong things,

Pushed Me To Do The Right Thing,

Even When It Was Hard To Do.

You Took Care Of Me When I Was Sick,

And Your Love Helped Me To Go Through Hell.You

Had Rules, And I Learned New Things When I Obeyed

Them, My Life Was Simpler,Better,Richer.,You Were

And Are ,The Guiding Light Of My Life.

My Heart Is Filled With Love For You,

My Teacher,My Friend, My Mother

Without You

Without You Mom I'm Nothing

Your love, Your attention, Your presence

Have Made Me Who I'm Today.Without You I Would

have Been Lost.Travelling aimlessly,

Without Direction or purpose You Showed Me The

Way,

To Achieve My Goals

Without You There Would Be No Me I Could Never Fill

that space

No Matter How Hard I try!!

I Have joy, Happiness,Accomplishment,Peace, and most

importantly Love

Thank You Mom I Have Always Loved You

And I Always Will.

MUSKAN SHAH

Muskan Shah is a girl from Jharsuguda a small City in Odisha. She is pursuing the course of Company secretary. She loves to write poems, short stories, quotes and letters.

Mom

Mom
The 3 alphabets
Taught me love and hate
How to behave
And be brave
How to be strong
And how to live long
My mother, My best friend
My super women, My other end
She is the one , who inspire me
To make me better with a good family
She know how I feel when silent
She know what is waste, what relevant
She takes care of the whole family
She is a lady with the cutest smilie
There's lot to write
But what to recite
No wonder she is great
But sometimes making me fat
Lastly I wanna say this mom
I love you, you make me feel home.

माँ

वह कहेगी नहीं दुआं पढ़ जाएगी, वह पूछेगी नहीं पर समझ जाएगी,

मां तो मां होती है दोस्तों बिना खुद खाए पहले तुझे खिलाएगी।

उसकी मुस्कान में तुझे जन्नत नजर आयेगी, उसके कदमों में दुनिया सिमट जाएगी,

मां से ऊपर दर्जा नहीं होता किसिका, उसकी मन्नतों से ज़िन्दगी सवर जाएगी।

खुद पहनेगी भले ही पुराने कपड़े, पर तुझे नया दिलाएगी, पापा से थोड़ा लड़ कर, वो हमेशा तुझे बचाएगी ।

पैसे थोड़े कम क्यों ना हो उसके पास, तेरे लिए खिलोना नया ही लाएगी, घर में भले हो थोड़े रासन की दंगी,

पर तुझे अच्छे स्कूल में ही पढ़ाएगी।

मां तो मां है दोस्तों, इससे ज्यादा क्या ही मै बोल पाऊंगी,

बस इतना पता है मां है मेरी, तो दुनिया मेरी भी सुनहरी नज़र आयेगी।

NILOFAR FAROOQUI

Meet our co-author Nilofar Farooqui Tauseef, basically from Bihar Sharif, Nalanda but staying in Mumbai. She is Software Engineer as her proffession and Wiring poems, ghazals, scripts, quotes, microtale, is her hobby. She wants to make a new changes in life by the motivational quotes or speeches.

माँ

कर लो कुछ भी खातिर उनके , माँ का क़र्ज़ अदा नही होता।

माँ गर कहीं रूठ जाए तुमसे, तो खुश कभी ख़ुदा नही होता ।

कभी हौसला, कभी दुआ ,तो कभी मन्नत है

माँ वो है जिनके पैरों तले जन्नत है ।

सुकून दिल में होगी, कर लो ये इबादत है

माँ वो है जिनके पैरों तले जन्नत है ।

इश्क़ का समंदर है, दिलों की राहत है।

माँ वो है जिनके पैरों तले जन्नत है ।

तड़प न होगी, गर दुनिया में भी कयामत ह, माँ वो है जिनके पैरों तले जन्नत है ।

कर लो यक़ीन, ये ही वो हक़ीक़त है।

माँ वो है जिनके पैरों तले जन्नत है ।

वो लफ्ज़ कहाँ से लाऊँ जो माँ पे लिख दे नीलोफर

माँ के लफ्ज़ में नही हर हर्फ़ में राहत है ।

माँ \ □□□ \ Maa

तेरी गोद में सर रखकर सो जाने को जी चाहता है, वही पुरानी लोरी में खो जाने को जी चाहता है।

थक गए हैं बहुत ज़माने की इस तपिश से, आँचल के साये में सो जाने को जी चाहता है।

न दौलत न किसी शोहरत की है चाहत मुझको, तेरे क़दमों तले जन्नत में रह जाने को जी चाहता है।

कोई अपना नही है, सिर्फ एक सिवाए तेरे,ये बात बार बार दोहराने को जी चाहता है।

क़ैद कर लिए न जाने कितने ग़म इस सीने में ,तुझसे गले लगकर खूब रोने को जी चाहता है।

लौटा दे कोई मेरे ,वो मेरे बचपन की गलियां तेरा हाथ में डंडे लेना और मेरा भागने को जी चाहता है ,मैं हूँ एक अक्स तेरा, ये मालूम है मुझकोफ़िर भी तेरा आईना होने को जी चाहता है।

ज़माने की थपेड़ों ने हर दिन ज़ख्म दिए हैं बहुत तेरे हाथों के मरहम से सर सहलाने को जी चाहता है।

खुदा तू सलामत रखना हर माँ को इस दुनिया मेंआज यही दुआ नीलोफर, मांगने को जी चाहता है|

Luv u Mom

PINKY RAY

She is pinky ray, bengali born hyderabadi nawab! pursuing her bachelors! She is a published writer and are a boxer with soft heart sometimes. Follow her on instagram @wordsbypinky

My mother is sweet you say, but did you made her feel sweet by your arrogant behaviour?

My mom is too picky you say, but do you know how much she cares about you?

You taunt her respect just to make yourself cool, but did you ever noticed yourself getting down by making her down?

But, yet she is mother, who knows how to love her child unconditionally!

No matter how betrayed she feels by your recklessness!

She still is ready fight for you!

Mom is a gift who donates her everything to run a blood, which she hopes will rule the world!

-wordsbypinky

She is the air filled full of love,
Love, which reaches to the core of the heart
she has carried for 9 months,
A souvenir by God to the planet earth,
which gave the rays of survival,
Rays which made us alive to be benevolent!
~mother

-wordsbypinky

PRACHITA ARORA

She is Prachita Arora.

She wishes to heal all those broken ones so she writes. Just one those ordinary people who loves to write.

Follow her on insta- @my_mini_tales

आँchal

तू हँसती रहे, मैं हँसाती रहूँ,

यूही तुझे बात-बात पे सताती रहू,

फिर तू रूठे मैं मनाती रहूँ,

मेरी बड़ी- २ कहानियाँ तुझे सुनाती रहूँ;

ना दुख हो , ना सुख हो,

बस जब आंखें खुले दिखे सबसे पहले तेरा रूख हो,

ना अरदास खुशी की, ना गम की छाँव हो,

जो भी करूँ बस मन में तेरे जैसे भाव हो;

यूही तुझे देख ये दिल खिले,

वही साँझ के रखूँ जो तू सिले,

और अगर आँखो में हो आंसू नीले,

जब भी रोऊ तेरा आँचल मिले;

एक तू ही है जिसने मुझे लिखा हैं,

मैंने सब तुझी से तो सीखा हैं,

माँ तेरे बिना ये संसार फीका हैं,

एक तू ही है जिसमे मुझे खुदा दिखा हैं।

Oh my darling mom,

Sorry for all the things I did wrong,

You made me so strong,

That I can fight with any Storm;

Oh my darling mom,

For letting me know my powers,

Growing me up like little flowers,

Will make sure to make you proud at some hours;

Oh my darling mom,

Thank you for always being by my side,

Telling me places to hide,

Just wanna let you know that you are my biggest pride.

PRANAV VIJAY DIXIT

Pranav Vijay Dixit, Residing in Ambernath, Maharastra, He is currently appeared for engineering. He participated in many Anthalogies, recently publish a poem in magzine name as TZP Tare Zameen Par, He writes poems,quotes and microtales also,he would like to play with words, he made more than 150 poems and quotes in Marathi, Hindi as well as in English language.. He achieve some certificate in tabla and he would also good in playing leather instruments

मेरे लिए मौलवी की दुआ है तू,

मेरे लिए आरती का धुआँ है तू...

नए दिन की सूरज की किरण है तू,

आने वाली रात के चाँद की रोशनी है तू...

उजड़े हुए दिन के धूपमें मेरी वह छाँव है तू,

बिखरते हुए रात के ठंड मैं मेरी एक ऊब है तू...

धरती के ऊपर अम्बर बना नीला आसमाँ है तू

मेरे सपनों को हकीकतमें बदलने वाली मेरी माँ है तू...

मेरी प्यारीसी माँ है तू...

PRAPTI

Prapti is a 17 year old girl who hails from the Cultural Capital of India, which is Kolkata. She, along with being an avid reader, is also a philanthropist by finding her home in the lap of nature. She loves photography and writing prose and poetry. Follow her on insta - @mavis_malfoy.

MY PRECIOUS GEM, MY MOM

God blessed me with a precious gem
She brought me into the world, she gave me a name
God blessed me with a precious gem
She taught me to use my brain
God blessed me with a precious gem
She was with me when I studied or played a game
God blessed me with a precious gem
She will always think I'm lame
God blessed me with a precious gem
She gets overwhelmed in my pain

God blessed me with my mom
I proudly write yours with my name
I'm forever grateful to have you
I love you!

RICHA CHUGH

Richa Chugh aged 28 years thalassemia warrior, from Faridabad, Haryana. Completed her Post Graduation in finance. A Published author who loves to ink her emotions and writes poems, quotes, microtales on different topics varying from social issues to inspirational musings and also interested in making handicraft items. A person with crazy mind yet a positive soul is apt to describe her. Contact her on, Gmail: rc.inkdiary@gmail.com Ig: rc_inkdiary

माँ

कुछ यूं मुझको तुमने जो सम्भाला था,
हर मुश्किल से तुमने ही तो निकाला था,
मेरे हर छोटे बड़े सपने को अपना बना,

मुझे सपने की तरह ही तो तुमने बुना,
ख्वाहिशों को मेरी तुमने ही तो रंग दिए थे,
माँ मुझे उड़ने के लिए तुमने पंख दिए थे,

मेरा जीवन कुछ नहीं बस तुम्हारी छाया हैं,
जो भी पाया, वो मैंने तुमसे ही तो पाया हैं,
गिरने पर हर बार तुमने ही सहारा दिया,

मेरी खुशियों में अपने गम को भी छुपा दिया,
हर एक लम्हे में मुझे जीना तुमने सिखाया हैं,
माँ तुमने मुझे हमेशा एक बेहतर इंसान बनाया
है।

<u>My MOM</u>

My shield of tough times,
My shelter of the hardships,
My MOM...

My patient listener
My active helping hand
My MOM...

My very first teacher
My always last resort
My MOM...

My always best friend
My permanent confidant
My MOM...

My companion in the low
My team mate in the challenges
My MOM...

My guide always right
My willpower to fight
My MOM...

My today and tomorrow
My now and forever
My MOM...

RITIKA DASGUPTA

I am Ritika Dasgupta. I'm in college studying psychology honours. I write poems and like photography. I have done summer internship from The Fortis Hospital while I was in class 11. I love painting as well and recently got certificate from NASA regarding the Parker Solar Probe spacecraft revolving the sun. I want to be able to help people in the future and work on something which profits them and helps them.

Mom
Hi.
Well I don't really know what to write here but this letter is me thanking you for everything you did and everything you are still doing for me. I am one of those kids who can't express enough gratitude to their mother especially when it comes to thanking them for just being them. Thank you mom for always being there for me. Thank you for tolerating all my drama and just hugging me whenever I cried. Thanks for staying up late with me during my exams. Thank you for everything. Thanks for attending to every shitty stuff I did and never complaining.

Thanks for supporting all my sudden decisions. Thanks for being this awesome example of strength and resilience and thank you for being the coolest mom. I can make a never-ending list if I keep going. You have sacrificed more than humanly possible for me and I can never thank you enough for that. I want you to know that whatever you did for me never went unnoticed.
You are one of the people I'm most thankful for being in my life. I'm sorry for all the times we fought and I've pushed you away

many times when the only thing you wanted was to help. I'm sorry for not making enough time to talk to you but I know that you always made time for me. I'll always be there for you when you need me mom, I may not show it sometimes but I will. I'm forever grateful to you for not only giving me life but also making my life worth living. I couldn't be half the woman I am if it wasn't for you. I want to make you proud mom.

I hope I make you proud one day. You have always taught me to push myself and to always dream big. You are my idol, my weakness as well as my strength. As I grow older I cannot deny the fact that one day , hopefully, I'll be a mother too.

My only hope is I can be as cool and amazing and understanding as you. I love you with my whole heart

Xoxo R.

RONAK CHAVDA

Myself Ronak Chavda. From Rajkot Gujrat. Graphic Designer as a profession. Love to be express my feelings through my pen.

माँ ये एक शब्द नहीं पूरी किताब हैं !!

ज़िंदगी में कितने गम आये कितनी ख़ुशियाँ
आयी,
हर गम के साथ माँ की ढेर सारी ममता लायी,
ढेर सारे प्यार भरे कुछ पल के सौगात लायी,
माँ ये एक शब्द नहीं पूरी किताब हैं !!
रात भर खुद जाग कर तुम्हारा ध्यान रखती हैं,
खुद भूखे रह कर तुम्हें पेट भर कर खिलाती हैं,
हमें तकलीफ़ में देखकर कितनी मन्नते रखती हैं,
माँ ये एक शब्द नहीं पूरी किताब हैं !!
बुखार हमें आता हैं रात भर खुद जागती हैं,
कामयाबी मिलने पर महौले में मिठाई बाटती हैं,
एक इंसान परिवार को जोड़के रखती हैं,
माँ ये एक शब्द नहीं पूरी किताब हैं !!
अपने बच्चे को प्यार से पालती पोस्ती हैं,
अपनी बहु को वह बेटी से ज्यादा प्यार करती हैं,
भगवान ने प्यार बाटने के लिए माँ को बनाया हैं,
माँ ये एक शब्द नहीं पूरी किताब हैं !!

RUSHIKA CHAWLA

A 16 year old sarcasm lover with dark humour pouring out of her poetry. sometimes is also found sketching and painting out her emotions with loud music blaring out of her phone. Has a superpower of vacationing on the couch with a good book and wild imaginations to live with.

Dear mom,
Its been years since dad died. We were lost in the beginning, you were shocked, angry, and emotional. I had to be logical while you were sitting there, crying and sleeping. It was heart wrenching for me to see you in a state where you were not the "Rani Laxshmi Bai" that I used to call you.
You were a living zombie. It was so disturbing that I almost lost myself. There was only thing that kept me alive; the only thought I had was that, "what would have dad said if I would have let you rest and suffer there, in that state alone." I gathered myself up and fell numerous times just to see you walking and talking like before again. I know you have been here with me every time I needed you. Be it the small fights I have had in school with my friends, my heartbreaks or my huge misunderstandings with teachers and others out there.
You have been here. How could I let you fall? How could I let the pillar fall? I couldn't. and in those months, though I was just sixteen; I felt a sense of maturity and responsibility that I wouldn't have realized otherwise. I know I have faults and I have done mistakes but I also know that you will always be there if I ever need you.

Not just because its your duty towards me but also because we have a bond that no one can break. I have always been good with words you know. Writing my feelings down; rather than

expressing them has always been my forte'; but I also regret not ever telling you how much your little acts mean to me, or how I could never say "thank you" without getting up the courage. I don't show these emotions like others. But I surely try to be the character you have spent years in building up.
I still remember the first time you asked me to stand up for myself. That was the day, when you scolded me just because I was weak in front of somebody else. I take time to understand things, and I took my time to realize that your arms and your lap are the safest place on this planet. you are my first, last and the most long-lasting friend ever. From admiring your courage to learning how to fight and take stands.
From feeling useless while you scold to feeling the eternal bliss when you praise. I walk in a rose garden without thorns with you. I look up to you like a sunflower looks to the sun. I bloom around you like lilies in the fresh water. You are like the fresh water to the wilting flowers. You are the first rain drop to a barren land. After all this time, I just want to say that "I love you" is never enough to portray my feelings. Cheers,

A small creation of yours.

S. K. NANDHINI

S K Nandhini belongs to mandya, karnataka. I have completed my ug degree of bcom in Bharathiyar university, Coimbatore. I love to read love novels, Nandhini refers to holycow and it refers to goddess ganga and goddess durga. I started my writings in instagram and my insta id - Lovely_girl_tweety

Mother is a special gift in everyone's life,
She is a first friend to every girl,
Her love is great,
Her love is measureless,
Each and everyone deserves mother's love,
Mom will be our protective care,
She gives her whole love,
She is the one who never hurt our feelings,
She faces lots of problems
arround society, but she never quit,
Mother carry us in her womb for 10months
with gentle care,
She gives birth with lots of pain, but
Her love never fades,
My mother was everything to me,
I love to play with her,
She feed me everytime, I used to sleep by
hugging my mother ,
When I was at the age of five,
My mother got sick ...
She never played with me after that
I became alone,
I got angry on my mother,
She tried to console me, but
Iam not ready to hear anything,
Everything was perfect
till that moment ,
Suddenly my mother gone to bed rest ,

Relatives often visited my home
I was very happy to see relatives, but i don't know why they often visiting....
Once forever she slept, i started to wake her, but it went in vien
Mother didn't wake up,
Everyone there started crying, but
I didn't.......
Suddenly they took my mom away
I thought she is going somewhere, but later i came to know that she never come back to me, even
Today I don't remember her face
Sometimes I really longed for mother's love,
While seeing other's mom caring
I feel like crying aloud, but
I couldn't even cry for my mother ,
I faced many problems without my mother's support,
I become helpless,
Everyone started to treat me as
They never liked me,
Obstacles made me strong and bold enough to face everything ,
Today iam able live alone, because of my mother, so
I love my mother to the
core of my heart

SAHIL SOURAV

A 1st year law student exploring his interest in writing. I write what I observe around me. Content writer and researcher. I fill the void in my life with caffeine and books.

The poems, stories we see in books are mere fragments or remnants of a person's thought or ideas but I believe the real poetry is the person himself.

I hope my poems act as a preclude to your world of imagination and help you find yourself.

The All-Rounder

Synonym to love,

Replica of the Lord.

A calming contemplation,

A sky of relaxing sensation.

You are the hope for a better tomorrow,

My shield in front of a big sorrow.

You are the mystic garden of bloom,

My doctor on a day of gloom.

You are the patience that I need,

My bandaid when I bleed.

The one who wipes my tears,

A calming melody to my ears.

Heaven to my soul,

Home to my eyes,

Oh my mother you are my life!

SANCHARI DAS

Hailing from the city of joy, Kolkata, Sanchari Das is currently pursuing her masters in English after successfully completing her creative writing course, besides working as a content writer. She has contributed to multiple anthologies and published her book of poetry, "Leisure", along with her novel, "Not Just a Love Story". Presently, she is a part of a writing community named "Scribbled Feels". She aspires to become a great author someday and inspire millions of readers through her writing.

Travel Backwards to My Mother

I wish time could travel backwards,
That could take me to my growing years:
When holding my hand you would stroll,
From the gardens to the shore;
When reciting poems you'd make me eat,
But I won't gobble and hear you speak;
When listening to your lullaby I would sleep,
And dream of the fairies of which you sing;
When running to you after every struggle,
Would sort out all my crazy troubles;
When crying will cease in your soothing lap,
As you will caress my cheeks with your hand;
When afraid I'd let down my tears,
And you'd repeat there's nothing to fear;
When lonely I would never feel,
For you would always be there to heal;

When I would believe everything you say,

For I hadn't yet learnt to disobey;

When like a shield you'd stand by me,

And to every lock you'd offer the key;

When darkness would fail to engulf the night,

For at the end of the tunnel, you'd hold the light;

When I'd have a home where I can always return to,

And not step into the house that's empty without you;

When after a tiring day I'd come back to a home,

Build with the tender love of a Mother's womb;

I still wish time could travel backwards,

And return me my bygone years.

SAURABH MADHAVRAO JADHAV

Known as Saurabh The SMJ, author, editor, youtuber, various poems and articles published in newspapapers and magazines in maharashtra, handwritten book 'prabodhan' and 'yashache kshitij' book is published.

You are my world, I am your son

Mom, I wish I had words to tell

U have shown me a peaceful heaven

and guided how to deal a hell

I just cant spell

What does you mean to me

Mom, your love is a gift to me

Mother`s love is the only true love

It is the only unconditional love

No matter what I do,

Just like you, i also love true

How did you find the energy

To do all the things you did

I am amazed by all your things

You made a plant from a seed

आँchal

I want to write a poem for my mom

I learned from you

What does mom mean

I learned from you

What does love mean

I learned from you

Love which is pure and clean

SHAIKH SOHEL

Shaikh Sohel A 18 Year Old Lad Hails From Bhubaneswar, Odisha. He Is A Writer By Heart. He Loves To Write On Feelings And Emotions Of Human Kind. Currently Pursuing His Graduation In Agriculture. He Gets Inspired By The Various Characters A Man Plays In His Entire Life. He Also Has A Keen Interest In Music, Especially Sufi Songs.

Hey maa,

SOME GREAT POET said that in this world he has written in many topics but he never wrote anything related to mother then somebody ask why then the poet said that who has given birth to us and wrote all the happiness in our life ,what can we write for her but I will give a small glimpses of how mother love is...the word mother is difficult to derive but she is the uncomplicated person in everyone life who can solve the complicated problems very easily. Most of the time we demand something we need to but many a times mother agrees on that or many a times not and we thought that mother don't love us it is not the reality what we thought about if mother denies something then there more love has been hidden on it and she knows at what time what thing her child is to be needed .we can't compare mothers love with any other love because the reason is the women who takes all the pain if her child during her formation to staying in the stomach of mother and till the delivery that is not easy .the pain a girl takes when she turned into mother is not easy. In this beautiful world the word love takes a significant role which defines to recreate or re-construct the person and soul who has broken or to heal the broken ones and this ability power we will found the most in mothers heart and no- where else in the world. In the glimpses of mothers love I will devrive about whole cycle of mothers life... In the whole life cycle from the childhood to the end of a girl she may has to suffer from many a problems and has gone through many a situation where no one can understand what she is going through. As she grows through many a responsibilities comes through her and among all these responsibilities the main thing is she faces everything without complaining a single bit. then after being married the responsibilities get doubled but it doesn't get over in the whole life cycle . sometimes we saw that many a families having personal grudges with each other but later we saw a mother/women/girl has come ahead and taking the responsibilities happily she bind the two families or person with help of spreading love towards everywhere. spreading love everywhere and taking care of everyone with whom she is dealing with in the family she will take care and take all the problems upon her and without complaining she faces it .there is a saying that in the world of fully biasedness the love of mother what we called unbiased.. mother name meaning stands for a never ending job where she only gives love,care ,affection towards his loved ones and without any means of selfishness. But return what we do by sending her old age house and thinking that we can't take her responsibilities but in opposite she do the same to you but I am sorry to say in whole world mother never do wrong with there kids maybe whatever his/her kid has done to her .she quietly happily caring with his child passes away. sometimes we can't know the value of person who played a valuable role in our life but in her absence we know what is the value of mother/maa / ami In our life...this what I can't describe about her.

.Ami I am missing u soo much..

Your Sohel

Never ending love and care

Having a positive side every where

Laying in your arms feeling like heaven

Dreaming of future and setting the goals

Giving her back to made it possible

mother this is you

the sacrifies made by u

making us stronger from yesterday

teaching us the patience of time to

making us beliving in god

till the birth to mixing the ashes in the soil

you never left us ..

o mother this is you…

SHILPA KAMBLE

An Software Engineering Student, who is devoted to write as much as she admires coding. Writing her heart out under the pen name of Meera, this 23yr old has portrayed different side of her personality. With love in her heart, logic in her brain and humour in her nerves she writes about love, relationships, social issues, short stories from fiction to her real humourous experiences that come with living in this world. Email at: tumharipriyameera@gmail.com IG: @_meerakebol

माँ तेरे आँचल से बढ़कर कुछ नहीं,यह उस रात पता चला था, जब वो दोस्ती के नाम पर मुझे, अपनी हवस का शिकार बनाने चला था।

माँ तेरी नरमी का एहसास मुझे तब हुआ था, जब मैं पापा की छूअन से भी डर रही थी, तूने मुझे अपनी बाँहों में समेट लिया,उस शख़्स के छूने से जो नापाक हुई मैं, मेरी रूह को अपनी पनाह में तूने पाक कर दिया था।

माँ तेरी शक्ति का एहसास मुझे तब हुआ था,जब मेरा दुनिया से सामना करना मुश्किल था, जब उस हैवान पर ऊँगली उठाना कुछ नामुमकिन सा था, वो आख़िर मिनिस्टर का बेटा जो था।

तू तब भी डटी रही, मुझे हिम्मत देती रही, बिना नज़रें झुकाए मेरा हाथ थाम चलती रही।

माँ तेरे दर्द का एहसास मुझे तब हुआ था, जब पुलिस हमें अस्पताल ले गई थी, मेरे टेस्ट चल रहे थे, पर तेरे निगाहों से आँसू बह रहे थे

लड़ रही थी सबसे, उन वर्दी वालों से,गुस्से से आँखें तेरी लाल थी, ख़ुद टूट के बिखरी थी, मुझे दिलासा दे समेट रही थी, आँखों में तेरे आँसू थे, मुझे दिलासा देते आँसू पोंछ रही थी।

माँ मैंने उस दिन मुझ पर तेरा यकीन देखा था, जब कोर्ट में मुझे हजारों सवालों के जवाब देने थे,

मेरे हाथ काँप रहे थे, और सबकी आँखे मुझे शक की नज़रों से देख रहीं थी। तू ही तो थी, जो वहाँ एक बेंच पर बैठ, मुझे विश्वास और निडरता से देख रही थी। माँ मैंने उस दिन तेरा ढ़ीठ होना देखा था, जब एक के बाद एक दलीलें पेश की गई, कभी मेरे कपड़ों पर तो

आँchal

कभी मेरे दोस्ती पर ऊँगली उठाई गई, महीने बीतते रहे तू फिर भी खड़ी रही, कहती रही तू मेरे साथ है फिर चाहे कोई हो या ना हो।

आख़िरकार तूने मेरे मान को बचाये रखा, उसे सजा दिलवा कर तूने मेरी हिम्मत को बढ़ाये रखा। माँ मैंने उस दिन तेरी ममता देखी थी, जब तूने ठान लिया था के तू मुझ जैसी उन हजारों मजलूमों की आशा बनेगी, उन्हें इंसाफ दिलायेगी।

मुझ जैसी कईं मासूमों के लिए तू खड़ी रही, उन सबकी आबरू की खातिर तू लड़ती रही। फिर आया एक वो दिन भी जब मेरी शादी की बात चल पड़ी, ज़माना फिर बोल उठा था,

किसी की हवस की शिकार लड़की, कैसे किसी के घर की बहू बनती, इस बात को सौ बार दोहराया था।

तू शांत रही, एक बार भी अपना आपा ना खोया था, तू कैसे जानती थी, एक निडर नेक वर को ही तेरी बेटी को अपनाना था।

माँ तूने कई चीज़ें सिखायीं हैं मुझे, खाना बनाने से लेकर, दफ्तर का काम सँभालने तक, क ख ग घ पढ़ने से लेकर अपने जज़्बात लिखने तक, अपने लिए लड़ने से लेकर अपनों का ध्यान रखने तक,

पर तुझे पता नहीं कि सबसे बढ़कर तूने मुझे ममता सिखलाई है, यह सिखाया है कि ममता होने के लिए माँ होना जरूरी नहीं, निर्दोष के साथ उसकी लड़ाई लड़ने के लिए किसी वर्दी का होना जरुरी नहीं।

यही कुछ तेरी सिखाई बातें जीवन में अपने साथ आगे ले जा रही हूँ। कोशिश यही करुँगी कि जिस तरह तेरे आँचल के साये में हम सब ने अपना घर बसाया, उसी तरह मैं अपने आँचल में वही ममता का पाठ सिखलाऊँ।

To all my close friends,

So I have a single parent, my mother. I conceded this fact from you, but maybe this was needed, maybe I needed the courage to open up about this and maybe you all needed to be a little bit older to know this truth. I never felt like I needed a father to complete a parent child relationship. My mom is as open-minded and cool than any of your parents are. But also is more strict in situations where it is needed. She is the breadwinner, she is a housewife, she is a beautiful elegant lady with a strong heart. I don't think I deserve a love like this. And I don't think having a father would have been any benefits either. I am way more than happy with what I have, cause I have as much as any of you guys have.

So don't say "sorry" after hearing about having a single parent. Say "They are a strong person to do this all alone".

And to you, my maa,

How do I tell you what you mean to me? My words aren't that great but you would still fall in love with them. I remember being a teenager, and screaming on top of my lungs "why don't you leave me alone? You won't understand what I am going through". But you never left.

You stood by my side when I first started walking, you held my hands for two hours straight when I cried over my first break-up. You screamed when you were angry at me, but then ordered me my favorite chicken biryani. You heard my harassment story and stood up against all the odds, you taught me to be strong when life wasn't fair to me, you taught me to support and help others. You, maa you taught me humanity.

Maa you are the best thing to happen to me.

You gave birth to a baby girl but mumma you raised me and made me a strong lady.

I love you from the core of my heart, and on one fortunate day, you will be proud of your daughter.

Yours crazy,

Meera.

SHREYA BAISOYA

Just an ordinary student pursuing literature still figuring out what life has in store for me. my love for writing has led me to this and I hope to achieve something worthy.

Hey mom,

My words will never be able to do any form of justice to what I've experienced ever since the day I was born. The women who created me and introduced me to this entire world can never be thanked enough. Yes, she is my mother the lady who's my inspiration, role model, mentor and best friend all together. She had an ardent desire to conceive a girl, also she narrates to me how she used to visit multiple temples and present this wish of hers. But I guess somewhere not hers but my prayers were heard because I was blessed with such a mother. I definitely might have done some great 'karma' during my past lives which in return resulted in me being born to her. Back in 1990s, a family's prosperity was equated with the their sons. In a small village of Delhi, she was the only daughter and the youngest one in her family but this fact never made her feel suppressed. In fact, she used this as an opportunity to outshine which made her apply for the post of a police officer. Yes, it took a tremendous amount of willpower to be a working women in an era where this gender was never given an equal status and that too into such a profession. She have had her own sets of struggles which were faced and dealt with gracefully, without giving up. She had never dreamt of getting into the police forces but her hard work and destiny both led her to this path. Her exams for this post were followed by an arduous physical training, which was back breaking to some another level. Several people backed out because of this and left the procedure in the middle but her passion fuelled her and finally she achieved what she aspired for. Also, she married a man of her own choice which clearly shows her approach towards life depicting that she has always lived on her own conditions. After that she had some other goals to acquire. She continued with her job and at a very young age which was in her late twenties she bought her own house which costed her an arm and a leg. Her only wish was to give her children the best possible environment to live in so that they can grow up and become beautiful individuals. She gave us the best lives which many people dream of, but this was purely because of her diligence. I would not be able to suffice her achievements into words. She carries on to live her life and inspiring me each and every day with the never ending chores she does. My identity belongs to her and I owe a lot to her. Proudly, I can say that even if I become fifty percent of what my mother is I will be the most happiest and content person alive.

SHRISTI MODA

She hails from a small city Raigarh, Chhattisgarh. Currently pursuing her Master's degree, a writer-molded by life experiences and a budding Travel Blogger and Social Influencer. She started her journey as a writer by writing quotes and one-liners on Instagram and Facebook under the name #KAHANI (STORY). An incident happened in her life which made her believe in "Tere Jaane ka asar kuch esa hua ki tujhe dhundte-dhundte mene khud ko paa lia." - Ravinder Singh . Follow her on insta- @an.esotericgem_

HAPPY BIRTHDAY MUMMY

I love you so much. Without you, I would never be here where I am right now .You are so strong, so compassionate, and so incredibly generous.Though you also gave me your bad habits like over thinking , being very helpful to others ,trust people easily ;still I love you. Right now, I am homesick and missing you while I sit a few hundred miles away from you. Mummy ,Thank you for every text to say good-morning and good-night. For loving me , caring for me , handling my tantrums , fighting with me and for everything, I thank you. I don't think you could ever hear that phrase enough.I appreciate you so much. I would be nothing without you. And you deserve all the love you give others. Its just that I don't express my love that often.You are the only person I can turn to when I feel like everything is falling apart. And even after so many fights I know you love me unconditionally.You deserve so much more than I have given you because of everything you have given me. I hope one day that I can pay you back for all that you've done, but for right here, right now I love you and I miss you Happy birthday mumma.

May this be your best birthday

Kehna tera jo na manu, Ek ajeeb sa dard hota hai

Aankhen bhale hi na roye ,Par dil ye mera rota hai

Mujhe bhi fikar teri hai maa,Par main kehta Nahi

O Maa Yaad aati ho

Dear Mommy,

For starters, I want to say how much I love you. I sometimes say it too much, the point where it could lose its meaning, but everytime I say it I mean it. You're my hero, everything that you do does not go unnoticed (even though you think it does). You make everything look so easy and do everything without flaw, it is incredible. Since I have gotten to college and being so far from you, it has made me realize how I could not live without your humor and guidance through these crazy last couple of moths. You have the biggest heart of gold who will always give the shirt off her back to help those you love and that is something I admire the most. Thank you for everything you do.

Thank you for the life lessons. Thank you for never judging me for any decision that I choose to make. Thank you for standing by my side whether I am right or wrong. Thank you for the unconditional love, I know there is nothing I can do that would make you love me even less. Thank you for being my moon, my sun, and all of my stars. Thank you for being my backbone. Thank you for being my shoulder to cry on, whether if your in the next room or 500 miles away. I know the words 'thank you' are sometimes as meaningless as the words 'I'm sorry', but I mean all of the above from the bottom of my heart. Lastly, I want to say I'm sorry. I'm sorry for all the times I fought with you when I was having a bad day and just had to take out my anger on someone.

I'm sorry for the years where I thought hanging out with my mom instead of friends wasn't cool, because you are the coolest lady in the world. I'm sorry for the times I have let you down even when you say I didn't

. I'm sorry I don't do the house chores that you ask me to do about 20 times and then yell when you ask me for the 21st time. I never mean to get angry at you or yell, and if I ever made you cry, know that from the deepest parts of me,

I'm sorry because I love you more than anyone could ever love.

I miss you mumma

SIMRAN VYAS

She is Simran Vyas. A lacking writer, she write the words she can't speak, She says- "Always remember no one is more important than you to you". You can reach her at – Email- popupsinmymind@gmail.com and instagram- @popupsinmymind

Her Cruel Life

Being Daughter:-

She was eighteen,walking as bride,

She wasn't ready,he wasn't her choice,For parent's happiness,she sacrificed,

Having a pure heart,that was her crime,

She fell for him & started caring for him at some point.

Being wife:-

He took her caring heart for granted, Harassed her every day and night,

She still holded her patience tight,

Considering her parent's esteem,she denied every right.

Being mother:-

For the first time she saw her daughter being harassed,

She believed it's okay, It's going to be alright.

It was the second time,she couldn't hold her mind,

Choosing her daughter's life over her parent's pride,

To buy daughter's freedom,she reached every height.

"Mom u did great Thank you for saving my life that night

I know it was hard for you choosing your daughter over mother

I must say I'm luckiest daughter and you are the bravest mother

I Love you MoM

THANK YOU LETTER TO MY GRANDMAA

To My Lovely MoM (Grandmother),

Hey Grandmaa, It's me your Daughter,Haan Haan I know your Granddaughter. But, I call you mummmmyyy so it makes you my mom na. Haina?

Chalo let's get to the point, There are so many thing I want to Thank you about I know i can't list out everything you did for me, But there are few things I want to mention them :- Thank you for loving me like your own daughter

Thank you for ignoring your knee pain to cook for me(for this I'm sorry too)

Thank you for kissing and caressing my forehead while I was sleeping

Thank you for taking care of me at the age when you needed care

Thank you for making me understand what is love

Thank you for replacing my parents Thank you for correcting my mistakes

Thank you for guiding me to the rights Thank you for teaching me discipline

Thank you for making my heart peaced one Thank you for hugging me when I was hurt Thank you for reaching me at my problems Last but not the least:- THANK YOU FOR LETTING ME CALL YOU MOM,

THANK YOU FOR LETTING ME KNOW WHAT IS MOM Mumma you did everything,From pampering me to scolding me at my mistakes, There's something I always heard "No one can take place of your own mother" I want to tell them How you took care of me , How heartily you loved me, How unreasonably you kissed me, How you became my mom, How you became my Bestfriend and How you became my Guide to this cruel life. I can't imagine my life without you. They say "God cannot reach everywhere,so he created mother" I want to dedicate this line to you. "I LOVE YOU MUMMA"

Yours lovely daughter,

Siमठं

SONALI SHARMA

She is sonali sharma from indore, a student of journalism and a writer as well.

"*Maa*"

आज कुछ पुरानी यादों में एक धुंधली तस्वीर मिली,

जो हकीक़त में रिश्ता तोड़ चुकी थी और यादों से मिटने ही वाली थी,

वो तस्वीर थी एक जादूगर की, Mr. India नहीं पर थी किसी mother teresa से भी कम नहीं,

वो जो pain killer का काम करती थी दर्द में, और थी fever में किसी parecetamol से कम नहीं,

जब चोट लगती कहीं तो मरहम बन जाती थी, दिल के घाव में भी एक दोस्त सी काम आती थी,

वो जिसके साथ जीने के कोई वादे तो नहीं किए थे ना ही कोई कसमें खाई थी साथ चलने की,

पर उसके साथ मरने के सपने ज़रूर देखे थे,क्योंकि मेरा जहान नहीं था उसके परे कहीं, वो खुद मेरा जहान थी,

प्यार थी, नींद थी, भूख थी ज़िंदगी का सुकून थी, किसी भी तकलीफ़ में जब भी मन घबराया था, मैंने सिर्फ़ उसे ही दिल से बुलाया था,

वो कोई wonder woman नहीं थी, पर किसी super hero से भी कम नहीं थी,

जब-जब उससे दूर होती थी, मैं कभी चैन से ना सोती थी,

आदत बुरी एक थी मुझमें, उसके बिना कहीं सब्र ना पाती थी,

फ़िर कुछ दिन बाद ख़ुद को समझाया,

जब कभी मन मुरझाया, उसे सिर्फ़ एक call ही दूर पाया,

वो कोई Cinderella भी नहीं थी, पर किसी son-pari से भी कम नहीं थी,

मत पूछो अब मुझे जीना कैसे आया, शायद फिर किसी भ्रम से है खुद को समझाया,

पर एक बात हमेशा सही रहेगी, मेरी माँ मेरी रहेगी,तस्वीरें कितनी ही धुंधली पड़े, फिर चाहें हकीक़त बदले,

वो यादें और ये सच कोई झुठला नहीं सकता, के मुझको फिर बच्चा कोई बना नहीं सकता,

मेरी माँ की आंख में वो जादू था, कि शैतानीयां भी हार जाती थी उसकी हँसी देख कर,वो माँ थी मेरी, पर किसी बच्ची से कम नहीं थी..

SUCHISMITA GHOSHAL

Hailing from a small city Malda, West Bengal, Suchismita dreams high to touch the sky. She is an avid reader, writer, poet, muser, scribbler, storyteller, published author, blogger, nature lover, social worker & a freelance model. She has completed her graduation in Zoology along with her advanced diploma in Computer Application. She has authored more than 100 anthologies as a co-author, most of them are in process of publication. Her debut book titled "Fields of Sonnet" will soon be launched.

Dear Maa,

I don't know how many times I need to mention you in a letter to get the satisfaction of loving you. I guess, my thirst will never come to an end but my wordstock will surely. My letters for you seem like a source tucked with numerous ineligible words failing to describe your worth, more to showcase my thoughts & the most to prove my love. Maa, since the day you've given me the opportunity to see the light of the world, you've already been the only God of my life whom I am & always shall be worshipping till my last breathe .

The things I've learnt, acquired, achieved & cherished are the precious gifts of your existence. I can't see anything without the illumination of your love, can't feel anything good if you're not with me , can't stand up alone if you don't support me & can't take a step forward in my life if you don't proceed further your hands for me. The reason for my survival is only you. I don't know what would happen to me if you wouldn't be able to stay beside me & motivate me for every second. Being the backbone for my energy, working as a pillar of my strength & guiding me just like a perfect pathfinder, you've emerged yourself as the angel of my life.

I can never forget how you've supported me whenever I thought of taking a risky decision in my life. From being a writer, an author, a columnist & then working for other magazines & websites, you've always shown your enthusiasm & moreover, never warned me from doing anything. You knew, attempting for something unknown was never easy but still you influenced me a lot to go forward. Same goes with my modelling career, where I've seen your clear interest to see your daughter presenting herself in front of a camera. All of these things were never a piece of cake & today, if I am going smooth, your contribution will get the highest credibility.

It's not like I never failed or felt disappointed or got down in my life, but their effect reduced to a certain point & became minimal only because I have a mother like you who can shelter me in her lap & arms when I'm flooded with tears or tiredness. Not a single day passed that you didn't look after my whereabouts in spite of running your hectic schedule.

The way I've always been pampered & all of my demands have been taken care of, I feel really blessed to have parents like you & papa. See, I told you that my words will get short of, but my feelings won't. I am clueless about how much I will succeed in accomplishing all the dreams flawlessly, but I can promise that I'll surely make you proud enough to say ," Yes, she is the daughter for whom I feel blessed." I love you more than the universe & hope you never lose your hope on me & keep on showering this unconditional love forever.

From, Your one & only daughter.

SUSHIL KUMAR GOCHHAYAT

Sushil Kumar Gochhayat is an eminent engineer rendering his services to National Aluminium Company Limited (A Government of India Enterprise), Damanjodi, Odisha, incumbent as Deputy Manager (Chemical). He is a logodaedalus and his penchant for writing has made him to produce many magnificent creations in literature that have been published in many popular magazines and anthologies proving his unparalleled excellence.

The best creation of God:

One who coaxes to eat more

though I say my belly is full,

one who remains

insomniac and sits beside me

when my ailing body

needs alleviation,

is none other than

the best creation of God,

my mother.

Yes, she is the epitome of love,

the Goddess of pure heart who discovers

her bliss in my happiness.

Yes, she is the selfless

and best creation of God

without whom,

I can't think about my life.

Unique and irreplaceable:

The immortal love for which even
God takes incarnation
and spends His tenure in the mortal world
is mother's love.
Mother pours selfless and endless love
from her bosom on her children
without bothering about herself.
Her lap becomes safe shelter,
her veil becomes the wiper for tension
and her cosy words
become the panacea
for all disease.
Yes, mother's love
is unique and irreplaceable.

SWADHA SINGH

In a garden full of flowers, she is not a rose you'd come lookin for. She is a dandelion you'd see dancing in the air not bothered of being seen. Swadha Singh, a 15 year old budding writer has been a permanent writer on mirakee for past one year. She has been a part of 10+ anthologies. As the writer is extremely close to her mother, this anthology is really close to her heart.

Dear maa,

The other day I sat under the Banyan tree pondering about something I had heard girls chirp out in school.

They talked of parties and pompous gifts they were going to shower on their moms this mothers' day. The substance was engrossing and I was translocated to a world where I imagined showering you with teddy bears and beautiful flowers. But alas, it didn't not last long. My pragmatic mind brought me back to a reality in which I simply couldn't celebrate mothers' day.

How awful it is that I can't even honour the one who gave me the most comfortable space in a part of her body, and allowed me to live under a sky glittering with stardust. People celebrate this day once an year. But maa, I've been celebrating it since the day I was born. Everyday I've craved to hug you so tight,everyday I have wished to sleep listening lullabies sang by you. I never got a chance to see your face but I know you were beautiful. I never heard your voice, but I know it was as mellifluous as the nightingale. I know maa.

I haven't planned anything for today. It makes me feel miserable. In the morning, I kept out water and grains for the birds. Their constant chirping in the morning wakes me up everyday.It compensates for the scolding I wish to get from you for staying in bed till late.

I watered the Banyan tree too. It hears my poems and stories just the way you would do. I cleaned my little house a bit extra today. It's warmth on cold nights is a recompense for your warm hugs.

I plan to sleep under the sky. I wish to accompany the solitary moon and listen him singing lullabies tonight. Every night it sings to me and makes me sleep comfortably on the rough mattress. I try smiling when the wind ruffles my hair. It feels as if it's your hands doing it.

I do these things daily. But the fact that I can't even hug you on mothers' day breaks me. I wish to shower youwith love. But i can't. Being an orphan is wretched. I wish I wasn't one, atleast for this day. I'm sorry maa for not celebrating one more mothers' day. Forgive me maa, will you?

The sky caught her mother smiling. Her daughter, who complained of not celebrating mothers' day had celebrated it in the most wonderful way. Her absence taught her how to value nature and every gift of God.

Her mother got the best gift. Her daughter was no more an orphan. She was in safe hands.

Mom,

It's been a long time since I wrote a letter to you. Technology and mechanisation have certainly reduced the need of handwritten letters but there are days when emotions overpower science and buttons of the keyboard turn futile when it comes to expressing feelings.

Past few years have changed a lot between us. The time that has flown by often makes me nostalgic. Touching my face swiftly, like a solitary zephyr longing for love, the past often brings back memories of us. Those days of kindergarten, when I used to come out of the school hoping to see you and no one else at the school gate brings back an innocent smile on my face. The 4 hours of school that separated us making me feel suffocated, or sitting on the colourful chairs, waiting and looking at the clock without knowing what it's hands indicated got lost behind the brumous sky of past.

The days of fifth grade when my friends came blabbering ill about their mothers, constantly saying how badly they wished to get a new mother, made me feel how lucky I was. Proud of you, I used to sit amidst them, listening to their complains of not being allowed to eat ice cream in evenings, or watch television after 9 o clock. It was not that you allowed me to do these things, but still that fifth grade old me knew that my mother was the best, and this fact was enough for me to not have any complaints against her. As my group of girls were done listing their displeasures, I would happily count all the things I loved about you, and conclude that my mom was the best one in the world.

Not many years have passed since those blissful days. But a lot has changed between us, mom. I know you feel it too. From telling stories and funny incidents of my classmates after coming back to school, to not talking to you for 3 to 4 days due to busy schedule, time has changed us. The present form of us isn't the mother-daughter duo we loved being a few years ago.

I wonder what has changed so much, that the things on which we used to agree just a few years back become the reason of heated arguments every next day. Have I changed? Or mom, have you changed? Everytime I ask this question to myself, the only answer I know is NO. None of us have changed. It's the cruel time. That little kid who used to cry leaving your hand at the school gate is still alive inside me.She can never die. I have seen you adore my childhood pictures. I've heard you whisper to the shooting star to get that little daughter of yours back. I have,mom.

I know how much I've pained you by not listening to the things you taught me.

Thousand mistakes I have made in my life and fifty percent of them were laid between us. Forgiveness would never forgive me for the scratches I've carved on your heart. But maybe you would. I no more wish to see you desire the five year or fifth grade old me. I want to be the best version of your daughter everyday. I want to be the one you cherish every moment. And maybe for achieving that,or for the sake of us,mom, will you be my bestfriend, again?

SWETA KUMARI

Sweta Kumari (gold medalist, M.A.) is currently a research scholar at Department of English, Magadh, University. Besides, she is a poetess and short stories writer, micro tales and quote writer from Bihar, India. She has been awarded with the prestigious awards like HONORARY DEGREE OF DOCTORATE, the universal Achiever Book of Records and Future Kalam's Book and others.She has a keen interest in reading and writing poetry and short stories.

Around Your Mother's World

As you are child, your world is your mother,

In all circumstances, you love to be together,

And keeping your head in her lap gives you enough relief,

Likely, around her, you get up, play and sleep.

As you are young enough, you wish to be with her,

To support, and to ease her burden,

But you know a mother's heart for her children,

Never get tired of caring and protecting them.

As you become enough responsible to hold,

You are more attached to play your role,

Whether it's about your family or home,

You are the one, without troubling others, want to take alone.

When from your bed after sleep, you get up,

When from home for work, you set up,

And then you return to your home being tiresome,

May be, for any reason, you are angry with someone,

All vanishes as you come to your mother,

As you realise that her presence is major.

TARUN AGARWAL

Hi This is Tarun Agarwal, he belongs from a small town Pali situated in Rajasthan,

He is an accidental engineer and incidental writer, Writing happened as a passion and a mode to express my feelings.

Instagram :- @writerstic

माँ,

कल जब उठा तो, देरी हो रही थीखड़े खड़े चाय पी रहा था मुझे लगा पिछे से कोई कहेगा ।।

खड़ा खड़ा मत पी चाय हजम नही होगा, दिल से आवाज़ आई ओर सोचा माँ ने यह सब बोला होगा, पीछे मुड़ा ओर देखा वहां केवल सन्नाटा होगा।

इस सन्नाटे को देख कर एक ख्याल आया, कैसी होगी मेरी माँ मेरे बिना मन मे यह सवाल आया।

इस सवाल के चलते एक मंजर नज़र आया, जिस आज़ादी के लिए लड़ा उसी पर सवाल आया ।

एक बार फिर से माँ से मिलने का ख्याल आया, दिल मे फिर से गाँव जाने का ख्याल आया। गाँव पहुचने पर माँ ने सीने से लगाया, और मै अपने आंसू रोक ना पाया।

माँ से गले मिलकर दिल मे हल्का सा एक सुकून छाया, जिसका एहसास बोहत अरसों बाद आया।

मेरे आने की खुशी माँ की आँखों मे साफ नजर आया, तरह तरह के मीठे पकवान का मेला घर मे उमड़ आया।

सभी पकवान थे मेरे पसन्द के, यह सब देख कर मेरी आँखों मे आँसुओ का ज्वार उमड़ आया।

घर मे बैठ सबने पकवान का आनंद लिया, पर मेरी माँ तो मुझे खिलाने में ही व्यस्त थी।

ना उसने कुछ खाया, वो तो बस मुझे खिलाती रही और कहती रही तू खा बेटा मैं खा लुंगी।।

यह सुनकर बचपन की याद आ गयी,वो पीछे पीछे भागा करती, और मैं आगे आगे भागा करता।

बस एक ही बात कहती तू खाता क्यों नही है, हर दम मुझे क्यू सताता है।

यह सुनकर रुख जाता और वो पकड़ कर मुझे खिला देती। यह और कोई नही माँ है।

जब भी घर देरी से आता तो डाँटती भी यही है, और पापा की डांट से बचाती भी यही हैं।

जब भी दोस्तो के साथ बाहर जाता और बिना बताए खाना खा आता, उसके बाद ताने भी यही देती, उसके बाद प्यार से सोने को भी कह देती। इससे आगे क्या बताऊँ, वो भगवान भी इस प्यार को तरसता है, तभी तो हर बार नए नए रूप में उतरता है।

सारे सुख हैउसके पास फिर भी, माँ के प्यार के लिए तरसता है।।

तुम्हारा बेटा,

तरुण।

TUSHAR RANJAN BEHRA

Tushar Ranjan Behera A Small Town Boy Hailing From Jatni In Odisha. Loves To Write And Is A Published Writer. He Is Currently Pursuing His Bachelors In Bioinformatics. He Also Has A Keen Interest In Music.

For Some She Is A Goddess

For Some She Is A Cute Angel

But For Me She Is A Support System

The One Who Cares For Everyone

The One Who Bears All The Pain

The One Who Loves Unconditionally

The One Who Does All The Tally

Never Bothers For Her Own Self

But Always Ready To Take Others Pains

The One Who Resembles God Herself

The One Who Embraces All Our Strains

For Others She Maybe The Reason Of Love

But For Me She Is The Reason I Am Alive..

Love You Maa

What Is Love ?

For Me Love Is My Mother. Who Always Tried To Cherish My Happiness. Who Always Tried To Give Me Everything Even If I Havent Mentioned Anything. Maa I Am Not That Good In Expressing My Love For Others.

I Dont Hate You For Whatever You Did. I Am Glad To Have A Mother Like You. When I See You Cry. It Just Tears Me Apart. Everything I Am Doing Is For You Only. Just To Give You At Least What You Deserve. My Anger Is Nothing But My Love For You.

As I Dont Want To See You I Tears Again.

Love You Maa

Your Son

TRISTRISHNA GHOSH

Writing had started as a passion for her, gradually turned into a hobby and then it became her daily dose of sleeping pill. Without writing she cannot imagine her life. She is a voracious reader and a scribbler cum writer. She has contributed her writings to many anthologies in hindi and english. She is a proud poet and author of 6 published anthology till now and many are in the verge of making. Her instagram handle is @deep.intodaylight

Dear mom,

Gone are those days of lush fields and greenery till I wrote to you. You might be wondering now mom, then why today? What happened? Actually here where I live, life comes to a standstill for few seconds. And that very moment I thought about my past golden days. Today I was thinking about you mom and your house, your gulmohur trees, the concrete bank of your river, the rain-filled potholes on your katcha road.

Did I forget to mention that I have forgiven baba for his continuous concern about my betterment and decision of sending me here? Oh! mom, You did not let me know whether this year's monsoon treated you well? Have your fields grown enough crops to provide all of you? Is my sisters still going to school at time and completed their basic learning of life lessons'? You forgot mom, or should I say you did not want to. I do not blame you. I know you could not. Ultimately I do not belong to your household anymore. You know mom, I am very worried about you all. I have kept aside some money from my earning for you. I know you need it.

Every time I eat mutton and rice, I remember those days of our starvation. You used to give us water and tell, "Have this my children, Ganga ma will fill our tummy, and hunger will not bother us anymore." I reminiscence about that togetherness. After selling me you have got 14000 rupees, did that fulfilled all your needs? I hope it did. At least money can solve some problems of your daily life than having a girl who is burdensome to your household. For whom you need to provide for.

You know mom, everytime here a chaos is created, always everybody is busy, dogs are getting in and out almost every part of the day. They all quarrel for my company. Don't you wonder how I became so lucky? Its all about destiny.

You know. I am writing this letter for one special reason mom, yes you are right, I have a reason. You know yesterday I went to market for buying some necessary items where babu da; yeah, the son of your panchayat head was standing with some of his friends. He pointed towards me and commented,

"She is the one! She is now a prostitute." And laughed vehemently. How can he say so mom? Did my skin has the label of prostitute in it? I don't know mom. So, if you know the answer tell me please. And mom, there is one more request, please tell baba not to send my other three sisters here, where I am, out of concern. Because this comfort will suck out the affinity towards life from them. If baba could not support them and give them food, strangle them with your own hands.

Believe me, in this way they will actually survive.

Only yours XOXO

By TRITRISHNA GHOSH(A LETTER TO MY MOM)

VANSHIKA CHOUDHARY

This is vanshika choudhary. She lives in gurgaon, haryana. She is currently doing schooling and is in class 11th. She likes to read novels, dancing, singing and listening music.

Dear mom

I want you to know that I'm really thankful to have you as my mom. I'm so thankful that I was birthed by a woman who is so strong and beautiful. You brought me in this world, cared for me, taught me, cheered for me and loved me. I'm also sorry for all the mistakes which I had done in my life due to which sometimes you got worried. I want that you never stop guiding and supporting me throughout my life time. You are my inspiration, role model, teacher, best friend and most importantly my all time chatting partner. I am so thankful to god who gave me a person in my life with which I can share each and every talk whether it be those funny laughs of mine, stupid talks mainly about my dreams and many more. You are the strongest woman I know. Without you I wouldn't be here. Even if I existed without you, I would not be who I am today. You have taught me how to be strong; whether it be emotionally, mentally or physically. There is no one else in this planet who I am closer to. I feels that I should become a reflection of such kind of a women in my life ahead who is so strong, beautiful, honest and an all rounder, and that kind of a women on this planet is only one who is none other than my all time favourite- my MAA. Thank you for letting me sleep on your bed when I was sick, for reading me a story every night in my childhood. But mostly, thank you for being a wonderful mother. Everything I do, is all for you.

With all the love in the world

Your daughter

Vanshika

VAISHNO SINGH

She is vaishno singh. Student of class 10th. She is currently studying in Daniel public school. She is from Jogipali Sambalpur Odisha.

Dear mom,

It's not easy to describe how much you are important to me . I always forgot all my pain while see your face with the happening smile. Your gentle touch makes me glow , your appearance gives me strength to blow. You are my beautiful rays of light who makes me Shine wonderfully. I know you always stand behind being my strength, being my backbone. Mom, you have given me the power to never give up in any tough situation.

Being My first teacher who who taught me the importance of gratitude and staying humble with everyone. You are my fall of Paradise from the heaven of love which I can't describe in millions of word all around the world . Mom , you have the hardest job in the world and you perform it even better each and every day with all your love and grace. Don't know where this much love you get from. Mom you are my role model can I be as great as you ? Here I am and who l am today is only because of you and I am so fortunate to have you as my mother. Thank you for encouraging me to never give up on my dreams and always being there and believing me. I am always be your little baby girl. Love you mom .

Your loving daughter

Vaishno

VISHWAJIT RB

Optimistic boy who finds happiness in others smile, lawyer to be, always looking to help and motivate others, joyful being who loves to cheer.

Dear Mother,

you are not mere human being but you are something beyond, and also not a person who should keep on serving our inferior soul.

You are the epitome of Love, Sacrifice and Mercy who is more Affectionate, Protective, and Supporting soul ever lived in the world.

You are Living God of the planet and maybe the whole universe who deserves respect and love.You are the positive force supporting me in every situation.

You pushed me to face new challenges and when I feel low, u consoled me till I forget the pain.

You celebrated happiness together whenever I was happy.

Ultimately u never let me down rather you taught me to rise again.

Thanks for this unconditional love of yours.

www.ingramcontent.com/pod-product-compliance
Lightning Source LLC
LaVergne TN
LVHW100845051026
849519LV00006B/2425
* 9 7 8 9 3 8 9 1 0 6 7 7 0 *